2012

To Carrie
Lots of love
Granny & Grandpa
XX

TREASURY OF CHRISTMAS TALES

TREASURY OF
CHRISTMAS TALES

PETER HADDOCK PUBLISHING

CONTENTS

FATHER CHRISTMAS'S LAST PRESENT

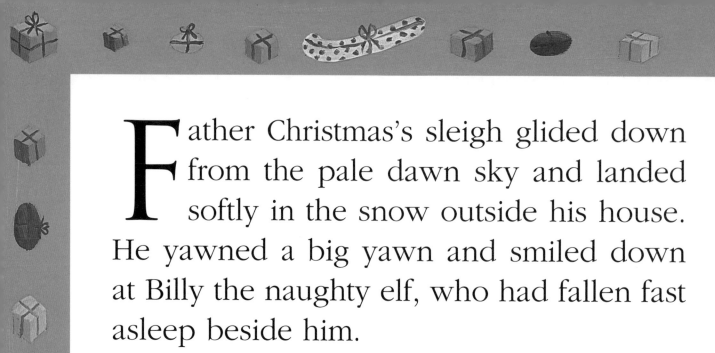

Father Christmas's sleigh glided down from the pale dawn sky and landed softly in the snow outside his house. He yawned a big yawn and smiled down at Billy the naughty elf, who had fallen fast asleep beside him.

It had been a long and tiring night and all the Christmas presents had been delivered.

All the presents but one!

Just then Mrs. Father Christmas appeared carrying a mug of hot chocolate and some mince pies. She gave Father Christmas a big kiss on his rosy cheek and carried the sleepy elf inside.

9

Father Christmas stroked the furry antlers of his weary reindeer.

"Extra fine hay for you," he said as some elves unharnessed them and led them away to the stables.

A creamy sun began to rise in the distance as Father Christmas looked at his pocket watch and smiled to himself. "Just in time for breakfast," he muttered and he put on some skis, pulled down his goggles, picked up the last present and set off. Father Christmas swished across the shining ice,

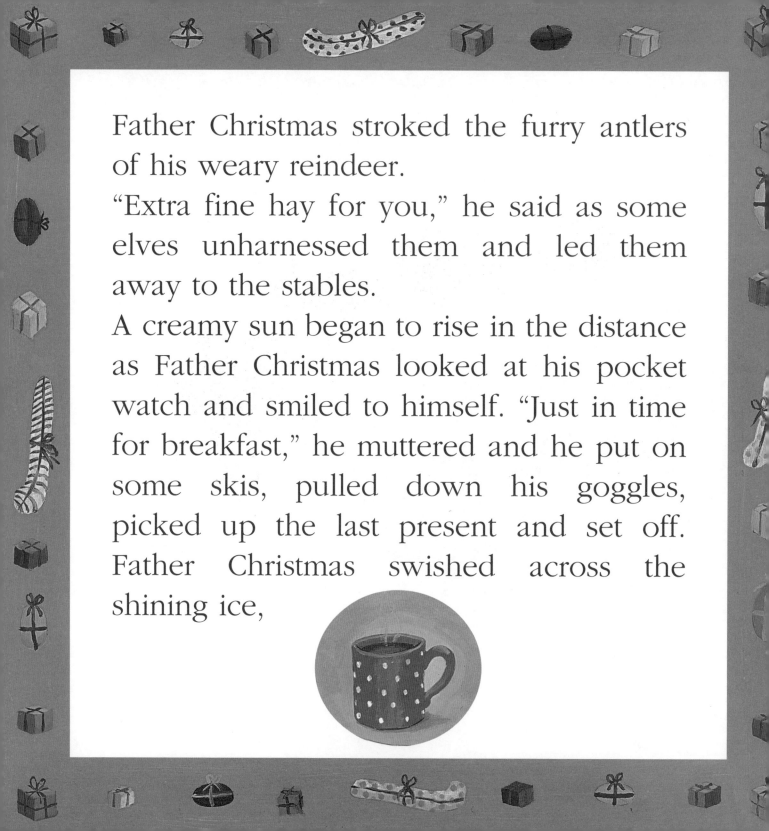

11

12

13

with his beard blowing in the wind. He passed a family of seals who waved at him with their flippers. "Happy Christmas!" he called as he swished past them. On and on he skied under the wintery morning sun. Soon he reached the edge of the ice where the great ocean started. A group of tourist penguins were ambling down the gangplank of a little package steamer.

When they saw Father Christmas they began squawking and hopping up and down. They pointed with their stumpy black wings and began taking photographs excitedly! "Happy Christmas," shouted Father Christmas as he whizzed past.

15

The penguins gazed after him with beaks gaping in astonishment.

Father Christmas glided on round the edge of the ice bay and round a corner.

The sun had risen quite high in the cold blue sky and the snowy land glittered as if it had been sprinkled with thousands of tiny diamonds. Swish, swish, swish went Father Christmas's skis until he arrived at an icy cave. He stopped, took off his skis and stepped inside the tunnel.

There was a great ROAR and the icicles in the tunnel tinkled like bells.

Father Christmas reached a huge wooden door and knocked three times.

17

18

The door creaked open and there stood an ancient polar bear wearing tartan slippers. "Happy Christmas" laughed Father Christmas as he hugged his old friend. "Ah, how lovely to see you" growled the mighty bear. "Come in, my friend!..." Father Christmas and old Polar Bear settled down by the fire and began eating a sumptuous breakfast of kippers and ice cream. Father Christmas told his friend about getting stuck in the chimney and they laughed and laughed.

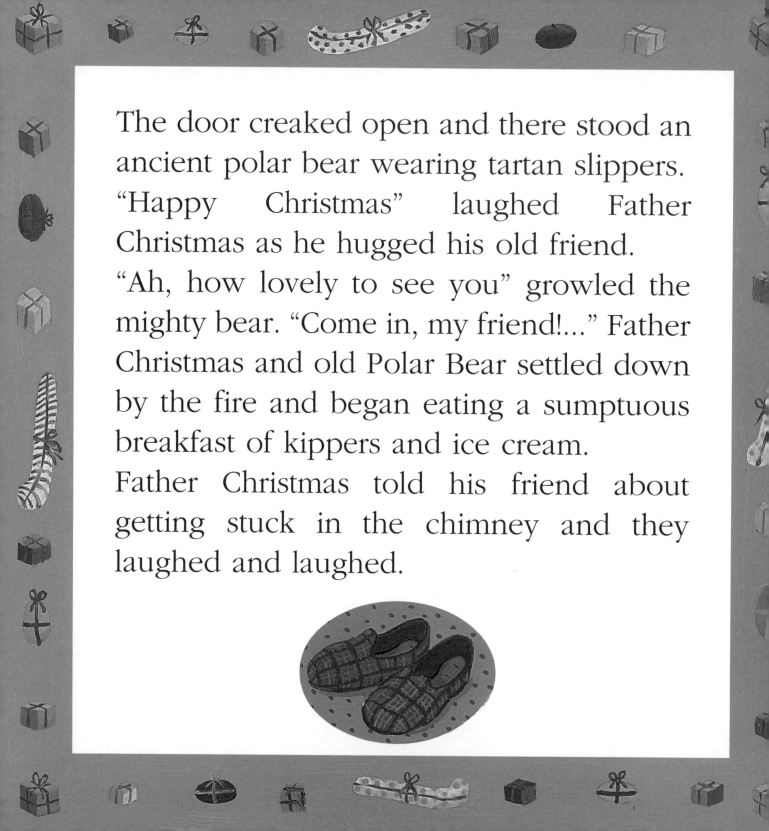

21

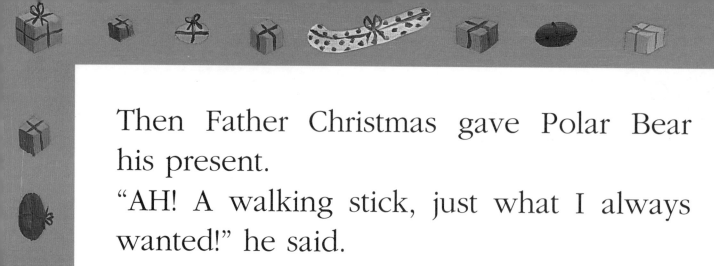

Then Father Christmas gave Polar Bear his present.

"AH! A walking stick, just what I always wanted!" he said.

"It's made from Norwegian spruce by the beavers!" said Father Christmas, "and I'm glad you like it!"

Polar bear shuffled round his cave using the new walking stick. He was really very slow but he said, "This is marvellous, look how fast I am going"

Then Polar Bear sat down to get his breath back. "I have a present for you too," he said and he passed

23

Father Christmas a large, lumpy parcel. Father Christmas opened it and found a strange, woolly hat.

"I knitted it myself," said Polar Bear as Father Christmas pulled it on.

"It's wonderful!" said Father Christmas, but they could both see how funny he looked and began laughing and laughing. In fact, they laughed until lunchtime when Father Christmas waved goodbye to Polar Bear and skied back home with his new hat blowing in the wind.

25

BEAR'S CHRISTMAS ADVENTURE

It had stopped snowing and the sky had turned a dusky pink. Bear was peering out from Charlie's warm, duffle coat pocket as Charlie and his Dad clambered back up the snowy hill, heaving the old wooden sledge behind them. Laughing children whizzed past as they reached the brow of the hill and turned to look down at the white valley below. "Look, Mum's lit the fire," said Dad, "I can see smoke coming out of our chimney." Bear stared up at Charlie and his Dad. Their cheeks and noses were red with cold and steamy air poured from their mouths as they spoke.

29

"Get on then," said Dad and Charlie stepped over the sledge and sat down with a crunch. Dad climbed on behind, tucked his feet in and picked up the reins.

"Ready?" he grinned and Bear felt the sledge lurch forward and hurtle down the icy slope. Faster and faster they went, bouncing over bumps with the wind whistling through Bear's fur. Suddenly, the sledge hit a bigger bump and snow flew up all around. Bear blinked, the wind had stopped and he felt very cold. As the snow settled again, he saw Charlie and his Dad in the distance, whizzing off down the slope.

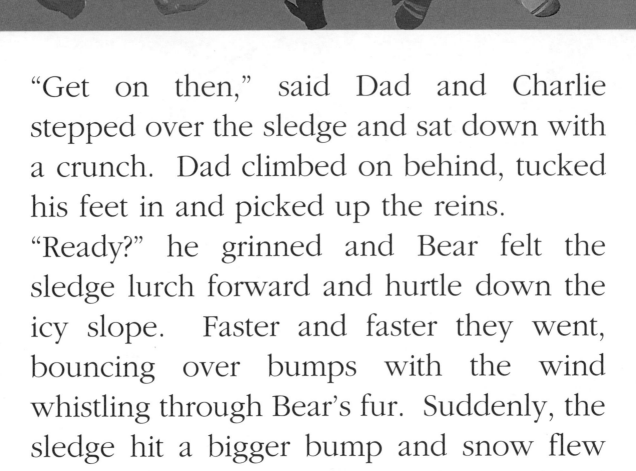

31

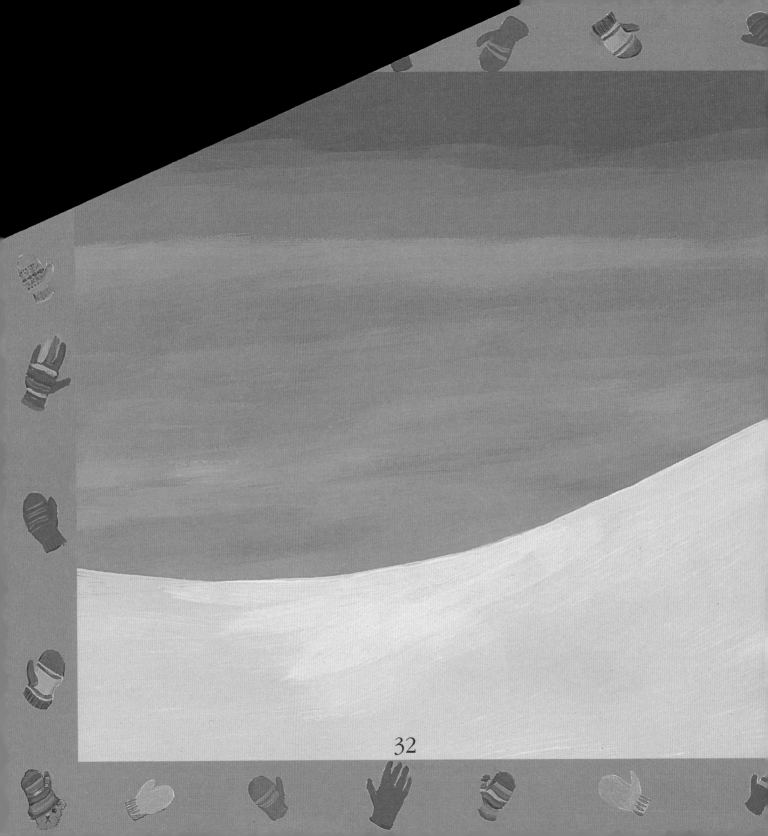

32

33

At first, Bear didn't worry. "They'll be back up in a minute," he thought as he dusted the snow from his fur. There weren't so many people sledging now and the pink light had faded. Bear stared down the slope, hoping to see Charlie and his Dad coming back, but all he could see was the orange glow of lights coming from the distant cottage windows.

"Oh, no," he thought. Bear stood shivering with snow up to his waist. He looked about and saw a stripey mitten lying on the ground. He pulled it onto his head and it made a perfect hat.

35

Then he set off walking down the hill. It was hard work because his legs were so short and he wished that he had a sledge to ride on. Just then he tripped over an old tray. "Ow!" he shouted and he sat down to rub his paw.

The tray slid forwards, Bear grabbed the rim and held on tight. He hurtled down the slope, launching into the air each time he went over a bump. He shut his eyes and waited for the tray to stop.

At long last, it ploughed into a huge drift at the bottom of the hill and Bear landed headfirst in the snow.

37

38

Bear heaved himself up and looked around. He could smell wood smoke coming from a nearby chimney, but he couldn't see a house.

"I must be at the end of the garden," he thought and he clambered up the drift to find the garden fence towering above him. Suddenly, Nelly the cat appeared, giving Bear quite a fright.

"Charlie's been looking everywhere for you," she meowed.

Nelly leapt down into the drift and landed beside Bear. "Jump on then," said the cat as she wiped the snow from her whiskers.

Bear stretched a weary leg over Nelly's back and held on tight. The cat leapt back up onto the fence and trotted along an overhanging branch. Bear could see the cottage now as he bumped along the garden path. Orange light gleamed from the windows and Bear could hear Charlie crying. "Now then," said Nelly, "I'm going to have to carry you in my mouth, to get you through the cat flap."

"Will it hurt?" asked Bear with a worried look on his furry face. "Don't be silly," said Nelly, "it's how we carry our kittens!" and she picked him up gently and poked her head through the cat flap. Inside, Charlie

43

was sitting on his Mum's knee, wearing pyjamas and sobbing. "Bear," wailed Charlie. "I want my Bear!" The cat flap creaked and Mum and Charlie looked around to see Nelly halfway through with Bear dangling from her mouth. Charlie slid down from his Mum's lap, wiping the tears from his cheeks as he ran. "Clever Nelly, you've found Bear!" he laughed. Mum poured a big saucer of milk for Nelly and Charlie started up the stairs with Bear peering over his shoulder. Nelly stopped licking her milk for a moment and winked up at Bear who waved his little paw and winked back.

CHRISTMAS AT THE
THE LIGHTHOUSE

47

Tom crawled out of his warm bed and walked over to his bedroom window. It had been a very cold night and there were icy patterns on the glass. He pulled on his dressing gown and gazed down at the shivering boats in the bay and the lighthouse perched on the rocks. Tom's Grandfather was one of the lighthouse keepers. Every morning as Tom ate his breakfast he would think of his Grandfather munching away on his toast and marmalade, up in the great lamp room at the top of the lighthouse. It was Christmas Eve and Tom should have been feeling excited and happy, but he couldn't help feeling sad, because this year it was

49

his Grandfathers turn to spend Christmas at the lighthouse. "I wish Grandfather could be here tomorrow," he said sadly.

"I know, Tom," said his mum, "I do too." At that moment bright sunshine and cold air spilled through the front door as Tom's dad stepped in. He had a huge smile on his face and his hair was all windswept.

In one hand he was holding a little tiny Christmas tree in a flower pot. "Another tree?" laughed Tom. "This one's not for us," replied his dad and he gave Tom's mum a secret wink and laughed.

51

53

Tom loved decorating the Christmas tree. His mum and dad always let him decorate it by himself. It was his special Christmas job. By noon the tree was covered in baubles, lights, stars and tinsel. Tom imagined his Grandfather peering through his telescope to see their Christmas lights twinkling in the distance. But, Tom was still feeling sad. He curled up in the chair by the window and watched as the crisp winter sunshine faded away and the first faint stars began to appear in the clear night sky. Then the lighthouse began to flash in the distance and Tom went to bed.

55

The next morning, Tom woke up very early. "It's Christmas!" he laughed and rushed over to the window.

"Happy Christmas Grandfather," he whispered. Then he got back into bed and began emptying his stocking.

Just then mum came in carrying breakfast on a tray and dad followed with an armful of presents. "Grandfather sent you this," said Mum as she passed Tom a small boat shaped parcel. Tom unwrapped it and marvelled at the hand carved, driftwood boat with its little red sail. Then he noticed the small label with a message from grandfather on it.

57

58

59

Tom looked up at his mum in amazement. There was a big smile on her face.

"I think it's time to tell you a little secret," she said. "Grandfather couldn't come here for Christmas so we're going to him!"

Tom threw his arms round his mum's neck and gave her a big hug.

"Now I understand," laughed Tom. "Is the little Christmas tree for Grandfather?"

"Yes," said mum. After breakfast they carried the presents down to the beach and clambered into the gently rocking boat.

61

In a few minutes they were sailing out into the bay. The calm, silvery sea glittered in the wintry sunshine as the little boat glided out towards the distant lighthouse. Then they spotted Grandfather waving.

"HAPPY CHRISTMAS!" he called as they drew up alongside the little quay.

Tom hopped out of the boat, ran to his Grandfather and gave him a big hug.

"I love the boat," he said, "it's fantastic!"

They carried everything into the light house kitchen, which was as warm as toast and smelt of roast potatoes.

63

"I'll have you know I've been slaving away in this kitchen since dawn!" laughed Grandfather. "It smells delicious," said Dad, "and you've decorated the room beautifully." "There's only one thing missing," said Grandfather, "and that's a tree, but they're a bit hard to come by out here."

Just then Tom remembered the little tree. He had left it in the boat. "I'll be back in a minute," he said and ran out the door. "Here you are Grandfather," said Tom panting, and he handed him the little tree. "Ah, wonderful!" cried Grandfather.

"This is going to be the best Christmas ever!" And it was.

65

66

THE BOY AND HIS REINDEER

One cold winter's evening, Saami's father asked him to go out into the forest and collect wood for the fire. He opened the door, stepped outside and gazed up at the sky in amazement.

He had never seen anything so beautiful. The sky glimmered with pink, green, purple and blue, like a vast, shimmering curtain of coloured lights rippling in the heavens. Saami knew that the patterns in the sky had a special name, "Aurora Borealis," he whispered.

Saami wandered into the forest and began gathering sticks.

69

Every now and then he glanced up between the overhanging branches at the patches of shimmering sky. It was getting quite dark beneath the trees and Saami had gathered a big bundle of firewood. He was just about to turn and go home when he stumbled over something on the path.

At first Saami thought he had tripped over a tree root, but when he looked more closely he saw it was a young reindeer. It was very small and had a hurt leg. Saami stroked the reindeer's head and looked around for its mother, but the reindeer was all alone.

71

72

73

Saami wrapped it in a blanket and tied it round him like a sling. Then he picked up his bundle of sticks and carried the little reindeer back home to his log cabin.

Inside the log cabin it was very warm and cosy.

Saami's mother helped him bandage the reindeer's leg with an old scarf.

"Poor thing," she said, "he looks very cold and hungry."

So Saami fed the little reindeer some watery soup in a wooden bowl.

The reindeer slurped it up very noisily and then curled up to sleep on a blanket next to Saami's bed.

The next morning the sky was bright and clear and Saami's father decided that he and his son should go fishing. Saami carried the little reindeer out into the sunshine while his mother packed some lunch for them to take with them.

The little reindeer sat on a blanket beside the cabin and watched Saami helping his father pack the fishing things.

Saami's mother came out to say goodbye and they set off towards the edge of the bay. When the little reindeer saw that Saami was leaving, it suddenly leapt to its feet and began hobbling along after them.

77

79

"He thinks you are his best friend!" joked Saami's father, "you should give him a name." Saami thought for a moment.

"I will call him 'Borealis", he said, "like the sky!" Saami and Borealis became very good friends.

They played in the snow together every day, until Borealis grew so big and strong that Saami could ride him through the forest when he went to gather wood.

Then one morning, Saami woke to find that his best friend had gone. Saami searched everywhere, but he could not find Borealis anywhere.

81

"He has gone to find a wife," joked Saami's father, "you'll see."

Saami carried on looking for Borealis but the days and weeks went past and there was no sign of him.

One year later, Saami's father asked him to go and gather some wood from the forest. Saami opened the door of the cabin and gazed up in amazement.

The sky was filled with shimmering colours. Suddenly there was a noise and Saami jumped round.

83

A huge reindeer with enormous antlers was galloping towards him.

It was Borealis! He licked Saami's face with his huge leathery tongue and Saami stroked his head.

Then Saami saw a mother reindeer and her young calf trot towards them.

Saami laughed.

"Father was right," he said.

85

86

THE DONKEY

Mary lifted the latch on the creaky wooden door and led the old donkey into the stable.

The hay on the floor shone in the late afternoon sunshine as the donkey ambled in behind her.

"My old friend, I have known you since you were just a little foal,"said Mary as she stroked his tufty ears, "and I know that you are really too old to go on a long journey, but tomorrow we must travel to Bethlehem."

The donkey looked up at her with its big brown eyes and brayed softly.

89

The next morning, at first light, Mary's husband Joseph went to fetch the donkey from the stable. He placed a leather saddle on to the donkey's back and carefully helped Mary climb up. She was feeling quite tired because she was expecting a baby very soon and Joseph wrapped a blue cloak around her to keep her warm. He led the little old donkey carrying Mary out in to the street and they set off for Bethlehem.

91

The pale morning sun glimmered just above the distant hills as Mary, Joseph and the donkey journeyed along the dusty road. It was still very early in the morning but there were many other people already on the road.

The day grew hotter and the donkey plodded on. Clouds of sandy dust billowed out behind his hooves as a warm wind blew across the land. By noon, it was very hot and so they stopped by the side of the road. Joseph helped Mary down and they all rested. The donkey lay down and nibbled at nearby patches of grass until it was time to set off again.

95

All day, they travelled along the dusty road until the daylight began to fade. In the distance they could see the small hillside town of Bethlehem. "Look, it is not far now," said Joseph and they began climbing the hill.

By the time they reached Bethlehem the donkey was so tired it could hardly take another step.

They arrived in the great square to find it bustling with other travellers.

Joseph looked about for somewhere to stay, but everywhere was full.

98

At long last they came to a small inn on the outskirts of Bethlehem and Joseph knocked on the door.

The innkeeper opened it and saw Mary sitting on the exhausted donkey looking just as tired.

"Do you have any spare rooms?" asked Joseph hopefully.

"I'm sorry," said the innkeeper, "there's no room."

101

The innkeeper was a kind man and he could see that Mary needed somewhere to lie down, so he led them to a nearby stable. It was really only a cave hollowed out of the ground where cattle slept at night. "This is the best I can do," he said apologetically and Joseph thanked him for his kindness and gently lifted Mary down. That night as the old donkey rested in the hay, Mary had a baby boy and called him Jesus. She wrapped Him in swaddling clothes and laid Him in a manger because she had no cradle. The hay in the manger was soft and warm and the little baby Jesus slept peacefully.

"Thank you, for carrying me all this way," said Mary as she patted the donkey on the head who brayed softly in reply.

THE ROBIN

untie Jenny knocked loudly on the door, her face grinning through the window. "I'm so glad you could make it," said Dad anxiously as he let her in. Emma and Jack rushed over to meet her. "Mummy's having the baby," they cried, jumping up and down with excitement. Just then the midwife arrived and Dad showed her upstairs.

"Come on you two," said Auntie Jenny, "let's go and collect some holly and ivy to make it all Christmassy for Mum."

They pulled on their boots and went out of the back door.

Outside the air was crisp and the frosty grass crunched under their feet.

Emma and Jack heaved the creaky shed door open and pulled out a wheelbarrow. They climbed in and Auntie Jenny wheeled them down the garden path.

"Hold on tight!" she said as they bumped from side to side laughing. A plump red robin whistled to them from the branches of a nearby rowan tree as the children climbed out. It followed them about, singing sweetly as they began snipping sprigs of holly and ivy from the hedge.

111

113

Before long, they had filled the wheelbarrow with spiky green holly branches covered in shining red berries. Emma and Jack pushed it slowly back along the path towards their cottage.

The robin hopped along beside them cocking it's head and singing.

Just as they were about to reach the back door, Dad flung open the window above them and called down. "Its a boy!" he smiled, "and you should see his hair!"

Emma, Jack and Auntie Jenny opened the back door and tumbled inside.

They took off their coats and wellies and washed their hands.

Then they ran off up the stairs leaving the back door wide open. The little robin hopped about on the doorstep for a few moments then fluttered into the kitchen.

Upstairs, Mum was snuggled up in bed with the baby in a big bundle on her lap. She smiled at Emma and Jack, who tip-toed over to take a look at their new brother. He stretched out his little pink hand and yawned. He opened his dark blue eyes and Emma stroked his soft red hair.

"He's beautiful," she said and Jack leant over and gave his mum a kiss.

"What are you going to call him?"

118

119

asked Auntie Jenny. Just then the robin flew in through the bedroom door and flapped round the ceiling.

Then the robin flew back downstairs and Emma, Jack and Dad followed it to the kitchen. The back door was still wide open but the little robin didn't seem to want to go out. It flew over to the Christmas tree and settled in its topmost branch.

Dad opened a window beside it but it still wouldn't go out, so Dad made Mum a cup of tea and took her up some fruit cake.

121

Emma and Jack decided to start arranging the holly and ivy and Auntie Jenny helped them make a Christmas wreath to hang on the front door.

The children wrapped holly and ivy round the wreath while the robin sang to them and hopped about the Christmas tree.

"Look," said Jack and he pointed to the robin who was tugging at a piece of tinsel. "He's making a nest!" laughed Emma and they watched as he pecked at the decorations and twisted the tinsel into a soft bed. Emma and Jack tied a big pale blue ribbon onto the wreath and hung it on the front door.

123

"Now everyone will know that Mummy's had a boy," said Auntie Jenny with a big smile.

The next morning, Emma and Jack ran in to see their Mum and the baby. They told her all about the robin building a nest out of tinsel and the wreath they had made. Dad helped Mum carry the sleeping baby down to the kitchen and she sat in a big chair by the fire. Dad buttered some toast and they all looked up at the robin who sat singing in his nest. "I think we've decided on a name," said Mum smiling at Dad.

"Yes, we're going to call him Robin!" laughed Dad.

125

126

THE CHRISTMAS FAIRY

Up in the attic, Angelica the Christmas fairy, was lying on top of a box of decorations, listening carefully. She could hear footsteps down below and the trap door suddenly creaked open. A pair of big hands reached up and Angelica felt the box slide forwards. She was very excited and she smiled to herself in the darkness. "Soon I will be sparkling at the top of the Christmas tree," she thought happily. Then suddenly, the box tilted and Angelica tumbled off. She landed on the dusty floor with a thud and the trap door closed. Her dress had ripped and she was covered in dirt. Angelica burst into tears.

129

She sat on the floor, rubbing her knee and sobbing, until she heard someone whispering nearby. "Why is she crying, Sylvie?" said a squeaky voice.

"I don't know, Berry," replied another, "shall we go and cheer her up?"

Angelic looked up and saw two timid mice peering at her from behind an old can of paint. "Hello," squeaked the mice.

"Hello," sobbed Angelica and the mice tip-toed over and helped her to her feet. Sylvie and Berry took Angelica over to the corner of the attic.

132

133

They crawled through a hole in the side of a big wooden trunk and Angelica looked around in amazement. There were little chairs made out of upturned teacups, a large book with a handkerchief on it for a table and in the corner, there were two beds, made from velvet slippers. Soon Angelica was sitting on a pile of letters, sipping tea from a thimble. She had stopped crying and was telling the mice all about what had happened. "Don't worry," said Sylvie, "we'll take you down to the tree."

"But I look such a mess and my dress is all ripped," said Angelica. Berry lifted the lid of an old shoe box and pulled out

some silver ribbons. Sylvie fetched a needle and thread and together they patched Angelica's dress.

She stood up and twirled round, swishing her dress from side to side.

"Thank you so much," she said as she hugged the little mice. Sylvie and Berry led Angelica down secret passageways that ran behind the skirting boards. On the walls, the mice had hung framed stamps and the wall paper was made of pictures from magazines. "Come along, Angelica," whispered Berry, "we're nearly there." They came to a large knot hole in the skirting board and peered into the room.

139

Sure enough, a huge Christmas tree stood beside the fireplace. It was covered in tinsel and shining lights but there was nothing on the top. A little girl was searching through the box of decorations, "I can't find the fairy," she called to her mum.

Sylvie, Berry and Angelica waited until everyone had gone to bed. Then they stepped out through the knot hole and began creeping over the carpet towards the Christmas tree.

They were about halfway across the room when they heard a loud "Miaow."

141

Frankie the fierce ginger tomcat leapt down from an armchair and bounded towards them. "Oh no!" said Angelica terrified, but the brave little mice ran and stood in front of her and shook their tiny fists at the cat. "Go away you hairy brute," they yelled. There was a loud rumbling noise and Frankie, the not so fierce tomcat, turned and fled. Sylvie, Berry and Angelica looked round to see what had made the noise and saw Father Christmas emerging from the fireplace.

"Ho, ho, ho," he said, "what brave little mice you are," and he pulled a little present out of his sack and gave it to them.

They unwrapped it quickly and found it was a beautiful set of dolls teacups.

"Thank you," they squeaked with their whiskers twitching in delight.

He gave Angelica a pretty hair clip with a silver star on it and lifted her up to the top of the tree. "Thank you," whispered Angelica shyly to Father Christmas.

She waved down at Sylvie and Berry.

"Happy Christmas," she said and they waved back.

"When you get back to the attic, you must come and have some tea in our new cups!" they squeaked and they disappeared through the knot hole in the skirting board.

145

CHRISTMAS
IN
SHERWOOD FOREST

Deep in the forest, snow had fallen for three days and nights and everything lay covered in a blanket of white. A wisp of smoke drifted up between the snow laden branches of a great oak, as Robin Hood sat, huddled round a fire with his band of merry men. "Come, my lazy friends," said Robin heartily, "we have much to do." He leapt to his feet and shook a snowy branch above their heads. He laughed as a cascade of snow showered down upon his friends, "Merry Christmas!" he called as he dodged a poorly aimed snowball.

Everyone was feeling very jolly, despite the freezing weather, as it was Christmas day and they were going to have a feast. All about the camp, the men were busy making preparations. Friar Tuck was kneeling beside the fire, singing to himself, while he stirred a large, bubbling cauldron of soup. Robin and Will Scarlet were carrying a deer over to the spit for roasting. Mutch the Miller was baking bread and making pies in a special clay oven.

151

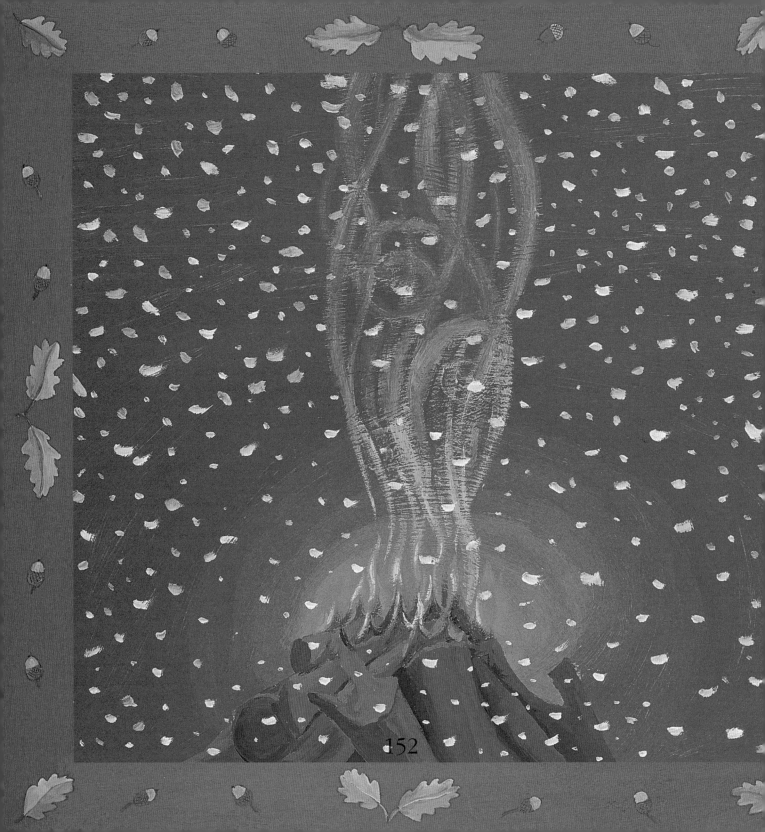

152

153

A huge, strong man with a bushy beard, who Robin called Little John, was heaving trestle tables about and whistling carols to himself. Robin rolled a heavy tree stump over to the fire and sat on it to catch his breath. He gazed around at the merry outlaws and thought how lucky he was to live amongst such fine fellows. Little John came over and slapped him on the back, "What's the matter, Robin?" he asked cheerily. "Oh, it's nothing," smiled Robin, "I was just thinking about the Lady Marian and how much I miss her," he said. "Be of good cheer," replied Little John. "She is warm in the castle and no doubt thinking of you."

155

Robin laughed and together they finished putting the tables out.

By the afternoon, the snow had stopped falling and the air was filled with the sweet smell of baking bread. Robin blew his horn to get everyones attention. "Friends," he called, "we thank the Lord for this bountiful feast," and everyone cheered. They sat down and Robin asked them to raise their glasses. "To absent friends!" he said.

The fire was roaring and the outlaws were warm and happy. Mutch the Miller sat playing his flute while Robin sang. Then suddenly an arrow came hurtling through the air and thudded into the great oak.

157

It was a warning signal and everyone listened in silence for the secret whistle that would follow. Sure enough, they heard a bird call coming through the trees. "That call means a stranger approaches!" exclaimed Robin and they all ran to get their bows and arrows. A few moments later the outlaws had reached the little lane, which cut through the forest, quite near to their camp. A carriage was trundling along through the snow, pulled by two horses.

It reached the place where the outlaws were hiding and Robin leapt out, startling the Horses. "Halt," yelled Robin, "no one passes through Sherwood without first emptying their purse." The coachman stared down at Robin looking terrified. "It is a cold winter and the poor have much need of your generosity," he continued. He stroked the horses' noses to calm them and waited for the traveller to appear, but nothing happened. The outlaws stared at each other in confusion. Then they heard giggling coming from inside the coach and heard a familiar voice.

163

"Hush Robin, you silly goose! It is me, Marian!" and she stuck her head out of the coach window. "Come and help me. I can't carry all these delicious dishes up to the camp by myself!"

They carried all the food up to the camp, threw some more logs on the fire and began the feast again. "I'm so pleased you came," laughed Robin as they danced by the light of the fire.

"I wouldn't have missed it for all the deer in the forest," she smiled.

"Happy Christmas, Marian," said Robin.

"Happy Christmas, Robin" she replied, as the snow began to fall once again.

165

FATHER CHRISTMAS
AND
THE NAUGHTY ELF

167

Father Christmas was sitting in a big velvet armchair, in his office, drinking hot chocolate. He was reading a very long list, which stretched all across the room. Billy the naughty elf was waving at him through the glass door. "Come in," called Father Christmas with a cheery smile and Billy swung the door open and hopped up onto Father Christmas's lap. "Oh dear, you've crumpled my list!" said Father Christmas but the naughty elf just wrinkled up his eyes and smiled his biggest smile. "Can I come with you on the sleigh tonight? Oh, go on, please, please, please, please, please, please..." he said very fast.

169

Father Christmas peered over his spectacles at Billy. "I've told you before," he said solemnly, "your job is here in the workshop, not on the sleigh." Billy slid down from Father Christmas's lap and sulked back out the door. The workshop was filled with busy little elves, wrapping and labelling toys. "Wrap, wrap, wrap that's all I ever do," moaned Billy, "I want to go on an adventure, like the reindeer, it's just not fair."

Back in Father Christmas's office, Mrs. Father Christmas had arrived with the big red suit. "I'm sure it's shrunk," gasped Father Christmas as he struggled to fasten the belt.

173

"Nonsense!" laughed Mrs. Father Christmas, "it's because you eat all those mince pies that the children put out for you."

"Well, I can't help it," he said shyly, "they're just too tasty," and he pulled on his big black boots and went out into the workshop.

"Time to load up the sleigh," he called to the elves and they all followed him carrying heaps of presents, to where the great golden sleigh stood sparkling in the snow. The reindeer had already been harnessed and the bells on their reins tinkled softly, while they waited.

"Where's Billy?" wondered one of the elves as they piled the last sack on to the sleigh.

"Yes," said another, "he should be helping."

175

Father Christmas climbed up onto the sleigh.
"Thank you for all your hard work," he said cheerily as he waved to the elves. He leant over and gave Mrs. Father Christmas a kiss on her rosy cheeks.

"See you tomorrow," he said as he shook the reins and flew off into the night sky.

Mrs. Father Christmas and the elves watched until the sleigh was not bigger than a tiny star, shooting across the sky.

Up in the sleigh, the wind whistled through Father Christmas's beard as the reindeer cantered across the sky. The bells jingled and the golden sleigh sparkled in the darkness. Soon they reached the first house and began descending towards its snowy roof.

177

178

179

Father Christmas looked at his list.

"Ah, Isabel, Amy and Lottie live here," he mumbled and the sleigh touched down softly beside the chimney. Father Christmas picked up his sack and stepped on to the roof.

He clambered into the chimney and was climbing down with the sack balanced on his head, when something terrible happened. Father Christmas got stuck.

"Oh goodness me," he said as he tried to wriggle free. "I can't move at all!" Father Christmas looked up at the tiny patch of starry sky at the top of the chimney.

A little bit of soot tumbled down and the sack wobbled.

All of a sudden, the head of Billy the elf popped out of the top of the sack. "Hello," he said with a cheeky grin. "Are you stuck?"

Before Father Christmas had a chance to answer, Billy had scrambled back up the chimney and returned with a piece of the reins. He called up to the reindeer on the roof and together they pulled Father Christmas out of the chimney. Father Christmas sat on the snowy roof covered in soot.

"You've saved Christmas," he said as he gave Billy a big hug. "If you hadn't come, I'd have been stuck in that chimney until next Christmas," he laughed.

"From now on," he continued, "you shall travel beside me on the sleigh and be my special helper."

Billy smiled his cheeky smile and hopped down the chimney with the presents. He was back in two seconds with mince pie crumbs around his lips.

"Come on," laughed Father Christmas as they climbed back on to the sleigh. "We've got work to do," and they swished up into the starry sky with the bells tinkling and the sleigh glinting in the moonlight.

LITTLE PUP'S BIRTHDAY

It was the day before Little Pup's birthday and he was feeling very grumpy. "It's not fair," he grumbled, "everyone else has their birthday in the spring. My birthday is on Christmas Eve and it's always freezing cold!"

"Oh dear," said Rabbit, but Little Pup just carried on grumbling.

"I wish I could have a birthday picnic in the meadow like Hedgehog," he said as he glared out the window at the gloomy sky.

"Or have a boating party on the duck pond, like Badger!"

189

It was time for Rabbit to go home so he said goodbye to Little Pup and hopped off towards the village.

It was very cold and as he passed the frozen duck pond tiny flakes of snow began to tumble from the sky.

"Poor Little Pup," he thought, "there must be some way to make his birthday special."

In the village Rabbit met Hedgehog and Squirrel so he told them about Little Pup.

"Why can't we have a winter picnic?" asked Hedgehog. "Everyone can bring food and we can go skating on the pond," added Squirrel.

191

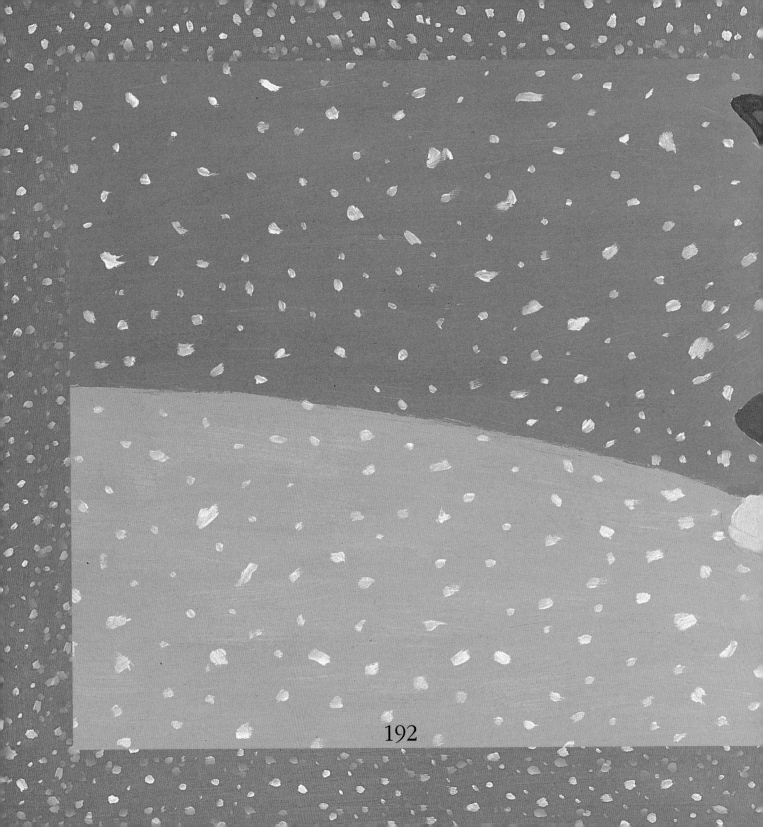

192

193

"What a brilliant idea!" said Rabbit and they rushed off to tell all the other animals in the village.

Early next morning, Little Pup was woken by a group of carol singers outside in the lane. He groaned and buried his head under his pillow. He stayed like that for a few moments then poked one ear out from under the pillow to see if they had gone. Little Pup listened in amazement.

"Happy Birthday Little Pup,
Happy Birthday to you!"

Little Pup jumped out of bed, threw on some clothes and ran to the front door.

195

Outside, the snowy street was full of animals carrying birthday presents for Little Pup. They all cheered when he opened the door and began singing 'Happy Birthday' again.

Rabbit hopped forward and gave Little Pup a new hat and scarf.

"Come on," he said, "we've got a surprise for you!" Rabbit covered Little Pup's eyes with his new scarf and led him blindfolded along the lane towards the duck pond.

All the other animals skipped along behind them, laughing and singing in the bright winter sunshine.

197

When they arrived Rabbit took off Little Pup's blindfold.

Around the frozen pond, the trees were hung with pretty flags and lanterns.

There were tables covered in food and a big bonfire to keep them all warm.

Little Pup was very happy.

Little Pup sat down on a big tree stump and began eating cake and opening presents. Squirrel gave him an ice skate for his left foot and a short time later, Fox gave him another for his right foot.

Badger gave him a home made sledge. Mouse gave him a trumpet.

201

Hedgehog gave him a telescope and Weasel gave him a deckchair.

"What a wonderful birthday I'm having," beamed Pup, "thank you everyone."

Little Pup carefully put his presents on the sledge and then began hurriedly lacing up his new ice skates.

The Mice Band began to play and everyone joined Little Pup whirling around on the frozen pond. They danced and laughed and fell over and got up again and laughed some more until the winter sun began to dip in the sky. It had been a long day and Little Pup was so tired that he had to be pulled home on his new sledge.

203

When they reached the lane by his house he climbed down and said,

"Thank you for my wonderful winter picnic, it was the best birthday I've ever had!"

All the animals cheered, and Rabbit laughed and said, "I wish my birthday was in the winter!"

205

THE CHRISTMAS PUDDING

In the cottage on the hill, Johnny wrapped himself in an old blanket and peered out through the frosty window. It was very early in the morning but Johnny was too hungry to sleep. Instead, he gazed down the valley at the towers of the Lonely Prince's Palace which sparkled in the distance. Johnny's tummy rumbled and he thought about the Lonely Prince and the magnificent Christmas feast that he would have in his nice, warm castle.

Soon Johnny's six little brothers came down for breakfast.

They sat round the table shivering and yawning as their mother carved up a small, dry loaf of bread.

She placed a piece on each child's plate and wished them all Happy Christmas. They thanked her and then gobbled up the food hungrily, until every last crumb had vanished. "Now, who will help me make the Christmas pudding?" she asked cheerily. "We will!" they shouted.

Johnny fetched the big mixing bowl while Mother climbed up on a stool and opened the cupboard door. The shelves were bare, except for a small wooden box hidden at the back. Mother passed it down to Johnny and together, they opened the lid.

SUGAR

FLOUR

212

213

Mother had carefully saved up enough ingredients to make the Christmas pudding! She poured in some flour, cinnamon, nutmeg, sugar, butter, eggs, currants and raisins and the children took turns stirring the mixture with a big wooden spoon.

It smelt delicious!

The children gathered around, in the warmth of the fire, while the Christmas pudding cooked.

All afternoon they waited until finally it was ready. Mother opened the oven door and lifted it out.

She carried it over towards the table but then suddenly tripped on the flagstone.

215

The pudding flew out of her hands, bounced on the table and shot out of the window. Johnny ran to the door and watched as the pudding landed in the snow and began rolling down the hill.

Johnny, his mother and six little brothers began to chase the Christmas pudding down the hill. The ground was white with snow and the pudding was soon covered. On and on it rolled gathering more and more snow. Soon Johnny, his mother and the six little brothers were all panting and exhausted, but they were so hungry that they had to carry on. Halfway down the hill they passed a wandering musician, an old man with a

217

218

219

three-legged dog and a fat lady on a horse who all joined in the chase.

The pudding was now a huge white ball that thundered down the valley. Everywhere, people came out of houses to see what all the commotion was about and joined in the chase.

Soon hundreds of people were pursuing the run-away pudding as it rolled on and on down the snowy valley towards the Palace of the Lonely Prince. It charged through the palace gates scattering guards in its wake.

It crossed the drawbridge and hurtled onwards across the palace gardens towards the massive oak doors of the Great Hall.

CRASH! The snow-covered pudding blasted through the doors and rolled inside just as the Lonely Prince was about to start his feast. It began to slow down, it wobbled and creaked and then came to a standstill beside the grand fireplace.

Everyone stood in silence.

The Lonely Prince stared at the enormous white snowball as it began to drip and melt all over the floor. Then he stared at the huge group of people peering in through the shattered oak doors.

223

He stood up and was about to speak when there came an almighty creak and the snowball fell open revealing the Christmas Pudding. "Who has made this Christmas pudding?" asked the Lonely Prince. Johnny's mother quietly stepped forward and curtseyed. The Prince took her hand and kissed it. "I wonder," he said, "would you care to marry me? I am very lonely and I love Christmas puddings." Johnny's mother liked the Prince very much so she said, "Yes." Everybody cheered and the Prince invited everyone to stay for the feast. From that day on Johnny and his brothers were never hungry again and the Prince was never lonely!

226

THE PANTOMIME

Daisy and Ben were very excited because Mum and Dad were taking them to the pantomime. Outside the theatre a great crowd of jolly people jostled about under the twinkling Christmas lights, waiting for the doors to open. There were posters everywhere and a lovely warm smell of sweets and ice cream spilled out into the street. A man in a black waistcoat unlocked the doors and clipped everyone's tickets. "We're in the front row of the balcony," said Mum as she directed them up the red stair case. At the top of the stairs, a lady shone a tiny torch on their tickets. "Your seats are over there," she whispered

229

and she pointed a beam of light to the front of the balcony. They were very high up and Daisy and Ben felt a bit scared as they made their way to their seats. They sat down and gazed around at the golden twirls that decorated the ceiling and the great chandelier which hung above their heads. The theatre was filled with the sound of rustling sweet wrappers and people whispering excitedly.

Suddenly, the huge stage curtains lifted and a beautiful girl appeared, dressed in rags. She was humming sweetly to herself as she swept the stage floor.

232

Then two big ugly women came tumbling in, laughing and waving an invitation. They were wearing very odd dresses and had enormous colourful wigs. They sang a silly song about which one of them was going to marry the Prince and Daisy and Ben thought they were very funny.

The girl in rags was Cinderella and she sat all alone on a little milking stool in the centre of the stage. She sang a sad song about her ragged dress and how she wanted to go to the Prince's Ball. Suddenly, there was a great flash of light and a beautiful fairy appeared. Daisy and Ben watched in amazement as she flew through the air in a cloud of glitter.

She landed gently on the ground and told Cinderella to collect some mice and a pumpkin. Then the Fairy Godmother leapt into the air, where she vanished in a puff of smoke. The stage went dark and everyone clapped. For a few moments nothing happened but then the lights came back on and the stage had completely changed. Cinderella was holding a pumpkin, in a beautiful garden with some little children dressed as mice. The Fairy Godmother reappeared and turned the pumpkin and mice into a beautiful golden coach pulled by four white horses. She sprinkled glitter all over Cinderella and her ragged dress turned into a beautiful pink and silver ball gown.

237

238

239

Cinderella hugged the Fairy Godmother and climbed into the coach.

In the next scene, the two ugly sisters were following the Prince around a ballroom and he was trying to get away from them. Cinderella appeared at the doorway dressed like a princess and the Prince asked her to dance. The ugly sisters didn't recognize her and kept hitting each other with their handbags. The Prince and Cinderella swirled around under glittering lights until the clock struck midnight. Cinderella gasped and ran out of the ballroom,

241

leaving one of her glass slippers shining on the floor. The curtain came down and Cinderella came running past wearing rags, with the children dressed as mice. When the curtain lifted, Cinderella was sweeping the floor again and the two ugly sisters were arguing about the beautiful princess they had seen at the Prince's Ball. Then there was a loud knock at the door which made Daisy and Ben jump. The Prince came in carrying the silver slipper on a cushion. Cinderella hid at the back of the stage while the two ugly sisters fought to force their fat feet into the delicate slipper. "Where is the foot that fits this slipper?" cried the Prince in despair.

243

"LOOK BEHIND YOU!" yelled Daisy and Ben. Then Cinderella slipped her little foot into the glass slipper and the Prince asked her to marry him. The ugly sisters fell over with shock as the Fairy Godmother flew down and turned Cinderella's rags back into the beautiful ball gown. The audience clapped and cheered as the performers bowed. The children dressed as mice came on in a row and gave Cinderella a big bunch of flowers and the ugly sisters threw buckets of sweets out into the audience. Daisy caught a hazelnut whirl. "Thanks for bringing us," she said, "it was really good fun."

246

THE SNOWMEN

One cold winters morning, just before the Christmas holidays, Rosie was sitting sleepily at the kitchen table with a slice of buttery toast in her hand. "I wish it would snow," she mumbled with a mouth full of crumbs. Mum came over and peered out the window. The sky looked gloomy and grey. "It might," she said smiling. "I heard it on the weather forecast."

"Really?" asked Rosie. "Yes," said Mum, "so you had better wrap up warm and wear your boots to school, just in case."

Rosie finished her breakfast, got dressed and brushed her teeth.

Then she put on her woolliest hat, her fluffiest gloves, her stripiest scarf, her furriest coat and her Wellington boots.

"I'm ready," she called in a muffled voice. "Are you warm enough in there?" laughed Mum. "I can hardly see you under all those clothes." Rosie nodded and giggled and they set off for school.

It was very cold outside but Rosie was as warm as toast. She skipped along beside her mum and gazed up at the sky for the first sign of snow. But none came. They arrived at the school gates and Rosie kissed her Mum goodbye.

251

Inside the classroom, she took off her woolly hat, her fluffy gloves, her stripey scarf and her furry coat and hung them on her peg. Then she took off her Wellington boots and put on her shoes.

Miss White called for everyone to come and sit on the mat so she could do the register. "Now then children," she said, "since today is the last day of term, we're going to have a bit of fun, making Christmas cards for our families." Rosie noticed that the classroom tables were covered in newspaper. On them there were pots of glitter, buttons, cotton wool, tinsel, paints, shiny paper and pots of glue.

Rosie was very excited because she loved making things. She folded a piece of card and began gluing a big fluffy snowman onto it.

"That's a lovely card, Rosie," said Miss White. "I love snowmen," said Rosie and she glanced out the window hopefully, but it still wasn't snowing. Then it was time for play. Rosie put on her furry coat, her stripey scarf, her fluffy gloves, her woolly hat and her wellington boots. She went out into the playground and ran about with her friends. Then, just as it was time to come in, the first tiny, white specks began floating down from the sky.

257

"It's snowing!" laughed Rosie and she stuck her tongue out to catch a falling flake.

Back in the classroom everyone was excited, even Miss White. The air outside was filled with huge, feathery flakes which tumbled gently from the sky, covering the playground. All the children looked out in amazement.

"Now then children," said Miss White, "have you all finished your Christmas cards?" Everyone said "Yes." "Well since it's snowing, I think we ought to have a lesson about weather, don't you?" she continued.

261

"So who wants to help me make a snowman?"

"I do, I do," cried the children. So they went back into the playground and began rolling balls of snow about. Before long the snowballs had grown so big that the children could no longer push them by themselves. So they helped each other. Soon, the playground was full of all kinds of snowmen. There were tall ones, fat ones, thin ones, funny ones and wobbly ones. The snow whirled around and children laughed as they added twig arms and stones for eyes. When it was home time and the parents began to arrive, they couldn't believe their eyes.

263

Children came pouring out of the other classes and stood with their mouths open, amazed at the sight. Mums and Dads laughed as their children pointed to the snowmen that they had made and Miss White took a photograph.

Snow was still tumbling down in huge, lacey flakes when Rosie's Mum arrived to pick her up. "I said it might snow," she said smiling, "but I didn't expect this much!" and then she noticed the snowmen. "Wow!" she said in astonishment. "Wow!" said Rosie as she spotted the lovely, new, wooden sledge her mum was pulling. "Hop on," said Mum and the Christmas holidays began!

265

THE CHRISTMAS TREE

I n the kitchen, Molly the cook was rolling out pastry for the mince pies. Little Miss Emily was sitting on the table next to her, trying to be helpful. "Oh Miss Emily, you have butter on your nose and flour all over your petticoat," said Molly as she wiped Emily's face with a corner of her apron. Emily licked a jam covered spoon and a big sticky blob dribbled down her chin. "I wish Papa was here," she said, "do you think he'll be home in time for Christmas?" Molly opened her mouth to reply but, just then someone knocked loudly on the back door.

She wiped her floury hands on her apron and hurried over to open the door.

Outside stood a man in a stripey apron.
"Where do you want it?" he asked. "Want what?" replied Molly confused.
The man in the apron pointed beside him and Molly peered out the door.
"Goodness!" exclaimed Molly, "come and look at this, Miss Emily." Outside, two more men, wearing stripey aprons, were carrying a huge Christmas tree. "This is number three Greengate Gardens, isn't it?" he asked as he examined a large receipt. "Yes, but I didn't know we'd ordered a Christmas tree," laughed Molly. "Well it's been paid for, so where do you want it?" he said.

271

272

Up in the drawing room, Mama was sitting by the window reading through a letter from Papa, which had just arrived. Every now and then she glanced out of the window to where her other children were skating on the frozen lake with Nanny. Suddenly, she heard footsteps, and Emily burst in to the room.

"A tree, Mama," she panted, "a tree is coming." Mama watched in amazement as the men struggled through the door carrying the huge Christmas tree. "Goodness!" she said, "I wonder who ordered it."

Out in the park, William, James, Charlotte and Annabella were skating about on the frozen lake.

Nanny glanced at her pocket watch and called over to them.

"Children, it is time to go home now," she said shivering, and glanced over the park railings and up at their house.

"Look, isn't that Emily, waving in the window?" she said and the children looked up and waved back. "She seems very excited about something," said Charlotte as they made their way home. When the children stepped through the front door they found Emily jumping up and down with excitement. "Come and see," she giggled, "come and see what's in the drawing room." They ran through and found Mama standing in front of the biggest Christmas tree they had ever seen.

279

They stared in amazement as cook handed out mince pies and mugs of warm milk.

"Where did it come from?" asked William, "did Papa bring it?" Mama looked sadly down at the letter in her hands.

"No it wasn't Papa," she said. "He has been delayed and may not be home in time for Christmas." When they had finished their mince pies and milk, the children began decorating the tree. Emily hung tiny silver stars on all the lowest branches. William, who was tallest, reached up and draped tinsel all around the tree.

281

The room was filled with the lovely smell of pine needles, the fire crackled and Mama lit candles. Outside the sun was beginning to go down and the street lamps began to glow. Mama pulled the curtains closed and watched her children finish decorating the tree.

"It looks beautiful," she said. Then Annabella walked over to the piano, lifted the lid and pulled out a tattered book of carols.

"Will you play, Silent Night," asked Mama, "it's Papa's favourite." They all joined Annabella by the piano and began singing.

"Silent night, Holy night........" Suddenly, Annabella stopped playing and listened.

Outside, they could hear another voice, "All is clear, all is bright..." sang the deep voice. "Papa," shouted Emily, "it's Papa!"

They ran to the front door and Papa struggled in with his arms full of presents. "Your letter said you would not be home for Christmas," said Mama as she rushed to meet him.

"You didn't think I'd miss Christmas with my family, did you?" he replied as he put the presents on the hall table and whisked Emily into his arms. "Have you decorated the tree yet, my little mouse?" he asked her.

"It was you!" laughed Emily, "I knew it was!"

285

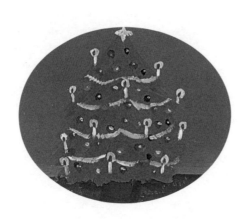